PLAYING WITH YOUR FEELINGS

by

EMPRESS SIMONE

To second chances and new beginnings.

Blaze

All will be revealed

Blaze was thrown for a loop. She couldn't believe the phone call she just had. She looked over at the man lying in her California King-sized bed. King was sound asleep, snoring peacefully. He looked like such a perfect angel. However, Jazzy just said that the receipts she sent via text message proved her thoughts otherwise.

The red drapes and Venetian blinds allowed a bit of the moonlight to creep in their spacious bedroom. Yet, the eggshell-painted walls started to close in on her. Blaze was starting to feel claustrophobic.

She picked up the red and gold wedding frame with their picture and hurled it at King's head.

"The fuck!" he screamed, looking around to see if there was an intruder in the room. King just knew Blaze wasn't stupid enough to do some dumb shit like that, but then her accusatory shrieks came out of her mouth.

"You are about a dumb motherfucker. Why are you still fucking Jazzy after all she put you through? Better yet, why even marry me if you were still carrying on with that ho!?"

"The fuck are you talking about?" King asked, scrambling to get out of bed in case Blaze threw something else, and he had to defend himself by choking her dumb ass up.

"You know what the fuck I am talking about, my nigga. Don't play dumb now!"

"No, I honestly don't. I do not even speak to Jazzy. All arrangements to pick up Junior are made through my mother."

"Yea, I bet!"

"You want to call her. I bet you she will tell you the same!"

"Of course, your mother will tell me the same. You are her son, who automatically makes her your ally. Please don't insult my intelligence. You know we have been through this before."

"Blaze, I swear I don't know what you are talking about. I haven't spoken to Jazzy in months."

"You mean you hadn't spoken to her in two days because Saturday when you were supposed to be hanging with the fellas, you were out on the town showing that bitch off. Why do this to me? As a matter of fact, just get the fuck out. I'm done."

"I will not get the fuck out. Especially since I don't know what's going on!"

"Here motherfucker look!" Blaze yelled at King while holding her phone out for him to see the pictures and video Jazzy sent to her via text message.

"How the fuck?" King let slip out his mouth, becoming dry from being caught in bed with Jazzy on video. He didn't know how Jazzy set his ass up so good, but she did. Now he had to try and sweet talk Blaze into forgiving him, or his marriage was finished.

"Blaze, I can explain," he started.

"Don't bother. I want you to pack your bags and get the fuck out. I warned you that it would be the end of us if you ever cheated on me again. You made your decision. Now I have made mine. I want you gone within the hour, or I'm throwing your stuff out on the front lawn. *And I don't give a flying fuck what these uppity neighbors have to say!*"

"I'm going to leave. Not because I want to, but because you need a moment yourself to process this. I swear that I love you, baby. I don't want it to end this way."

"Well, you should have thought of loving me before jumping in the bed with your baby's mother. I mean, come on. I love you too, but I can't do this anymore," Blaze said, feeling dejected. However, she felt good that she didn't have to fight King and throw his stuff on the lawn. The last time she did, it was embarrassing, but she remembered a saying her grandmother used to tell her, "*No matter how hard you try to hide your dirty secrets, all will be revealed.*"

King

I'm a Man

"There's *no way to lie out of this situation. I'm busted, and that's facts,"* King thought to himself as he pulled himself together to leave before Blaze thought twice about the situation and hit him upside his head again. In his mind, it was only one time since Blaze found out he was cheating with Isha. That was a little less than a year ago, and he's been faithful since then.

King also knew in his heart he was wrong, but he knew that given time and space, Blaze would take him back. He thought of all the women he had before and during their relationships, the outside baby had with Jazzy, and the time he married Neta before marrying her. The marriage lasted three months because Neta wanted to wear the pants. Plus, she wasn't the ride-or-die chick he thought she was. They got into an altercation once, and she called the police on him. In this day and time, the way they were killing black folks unnecessarily calling the cops was a no, no. Yet Neta didn't care. Even crying about Eric Garner being choked to death by the pigs, she still had the guts to pick up the phone and dial 911 because he choked her ass up during an argument. Blaze would never.

It took many begging and fancy gifts, but Blaze put that behind them and got back together with him. Then there was Plush. The one Blaze never found out about it. That affair happened during Blaze and his engagement period. Plush was dope. She had a dark chocolate complexion, curly hair that fell just below shoulder length, and a body like Bernice Burgos. But she had flaws. She hated to cook, she was lazy, and for a person who stayed home all day, her apartment should have been in cleaner conditions. Yet a dude would walk around in his crisp white socks only for the bottoms to become dirty. As a result, he always had to spend money feeding the two of them, and it was nothing worse than great sex than having to wait for the Chinese delivery person because the baby girl couldn't even make a proper turkey and cheese sandwich. So, King living up to his name, decided Blaze fit the criteria of the woman he wanted to make his wife and pushed up their wedding date.

Jazzy was hurt beyond tears and always threw in his face that he left her with a baby.

"I'm a man first and foremost," he once told her during a heated argument. "You are not a single mother because I take care of my responsibilities. Junior doesn't want anything. Besides the court-ordered child support I pay on time, I still come out of pocket for little dude and your expenses, for that matter. I mean, what more do you want?"

"*Commitment,*" she yelled.

"I can't give you that, and you know it. I'm married to Blaze now."

"But are you happy?"

"Yes, and why the fuck does it matter? I just told you I couldn't give you what you want, but I can and will take care of my son."

"Well, maybe you shouldn't see your son if you can't respect the person who gave birth to him."

"Bitch, there's not a place on God's green earth you can hide with my son. You try and take my son from me and see if I don't fuck your ass up, and I mean that shit."

"Whatever," Jazzy replied before picking up Junior and rushing to open the door so King could leave.

"Yea, whatever but don't ever try and threaten me with taking my child or,"

"Or what?" Jazzy interrupted.

"Try some slick shit and find out," King declared, then kissed Junior on his forehead and left out the apartment.

Jazzy was a bit crazy, but she wasn't stupid. She knew by the look in King's brown eyes that he was serious. She made a mental note that if she wanted to live in peace with her child, she'd never make the mistake of threatening to take Junior away from King again.

Blaze

In Hindsight

"Tee, I swear I can't take any more of King's shit," Blaze complained over the phone to her best friend.

"Girl, you say this shit every time something goes wrong. Stop lying. You will never leave him. He must have the dick of gold."

"Yea, he's packing alright, but that man must have some demon dick. It's like I'm possessed by him sometimes, but I swear this time I'm over it, girl. I've got to do better."

"You are doing just fine. It's his ass that needs to do better. As much as you have been through with him, he still turns around and does some dumb shit like fucking Jazzy. Girl, you need to move on this time truly."

"I will."

"That's what your mouth says now, but I know in a few weeks he will be back home, and I won't hear from you until the next time he does some dumb shit."

"Now you are the one lying. You know I speak to you daily."

"Not after you two make up after a break-up. Girl, you go in hermit mode, but no worries. I'm used to it. I mean, he is your man. I ain't fucking you, so I get it."

"He's my husband, Tee. My husband. We took an oath before God. I honor that oath. I just wish he did."

"You are too young to go through all of this, but he's the first man you ever slept with. So again, I get it, but he needs to remember the oath you both took and stop sticking his dick in every chick walking."

Blaze went quiet, knowing that her best friend was correct. She was willing to walk the extra mile for King, but he just didn't prove he was worthy or loved her as much as she did him. She was at her wit's end. Not only did he have an outside child with Jazzy, but there were numerous affairs she found out about. Some she didn't even bother to speak on because, as Tee reminded her, she was going to remain King's lady anyway.

"Hello, are you still there?" Tee asked, suddenly worried by Blaze's silence.

"Yes, I'm still here. I'm just thinking about everything you said."

"Well, don't overthink things. It is what it is. At the end of the day, a man's only going to do what we allow them to get away with. You've let him get away with too much. At this point, you just need to admit you will always have Sister-wives. If that's not how you pictured your marriage to be, then girl, you need to divorce him. First boyfriend or husband, it really doesn't matter. No woman deserves her heartbroken every other week."

"You are right, Tee. In hindsight, I see that he couldn't possibly love me the way that I love him. The only thing to do now is finding the strength to stay gone and dissolve the marriage."

"You can do it, Blaze, but be strong, girl. Little Darius is crying. He must be hungry. Let me go feed him."

"Alright, girl. I love you."

"Love you too. And remember, don't overthink things, just gather up the strength and move on," Tee reminded Blaze, then hung up without waiting for a reply.

"It's *so hard, but I have to be strong,"* Blaze scolded herself, then went and laid in the bed without eating or showering. She fell into an uneasy sleep where she dreamed of King and Jazzy having a threesome with another girl who looked familiar, but she couldn't remember her name. "I'll *kill him,"* she woke up disturbed and started crying. Hindsight was twenty, twenty, but foresight was everything.

King

The Shoot-out

King looked in the mirror of the hotel room he was renting at the Hilton.

He decided not to rent a studio apartment because he was confident it

would allow him back home.

King admired how handsome he was. His gold grill was sparkling, and the

turmeric soap he was using on his face had his brown skin glowing.

King's hair was in a low tapered cut, but he thought about growing it out for braids. In the meantime, he slapped on a fitted cap to accentuate his denim outfit. On his feet, he wore the latest Yeezy's. He usually didn't walk around with a lot of jewelry but tonight was a special occasion, so he wore his iced-out Glock-nine piece, a herringbone chain, and his Rolex watch.

It was his cousin's thirtieth birthday. They were going to the hottest spot in Phoenix to celebrate. They planned to go to an after-hours, underground strip club where there weren't any rules involved. They could touch the ladies all over their bodies and even pay for the head if the need called for it. Welcoming his cousin to his dirty thirties was going to be fun. Any problems he had with his wife were pushed to the back of his mind. Tonight, he was full of adrenaline, and he was going to let some steam off.

"Ayo man, are you ready?" his cousin Darnell asked over the phone. "I'm about ten minutes away. Don't have me downstairs waiting too long."

"Yeah, nigga, I'm ready. I'll meet you downstairs as a matter of fact."

"Alright."

The phone disconnected. King took one last look in the mirror. He was a fly; handsome brother and his swag was on one hundred.

Darnell pulled up in a range rover about five minutes after King reached the lobby exit. He hopped on the passenger side and noticed the two ladies in the back seat. They weren't ugly, but they weren't Blaze either. King wasn't expecting this.

"Yo, how the fuck you bring sand to the beach Dee?" he asked, annoyed.

"What?" one of the girls chimed in.

"I'm not talking to you," King warned her.

"Yo chill Honey," Darnell demanded. "Listen, this is business. Nothing more, nothing less."

"Business, huh? What kind of business?"
"I got three marks set up for the night. The ladies are just going to take back what's rightfully mine without it leading back to us."

"Us? I do not have shit to do with this, Dee. My businesses are now legit. I'm an entrepreneur. I don't need this bullshit in my life. And why are you still robbing niggas and not just coming to work for me?"

"Aye, well, I'm not into that slow money. I need mine fast and easy."

"What are you going to do at retirement age? You haven't paid any taxes?" King asked suddenly in father mode.

"Listen, it's my motherfucking birthday. You can save all that preaching you are doing for another day."

"Yea, you right, but just know, I'm not going to stop preaching until you get on the straight and narrow road. The lifestyle you are leading will only lead to death, and you have three children to feed."

"Yo, chill with that Creflo Dollar!" Darnell said, causing everyone in the vehicle to laugh.

The group headed to the club. They listened to the radio and were bobbing their heads to the music. Once there, King led the way to the V.I.P. room he rented, then gave directives to the bottle ladies on what champagnes and liquors the crew would drink.

Darnell spoke with the two ladies on the side. Afterward, he told King he'd be right back. Darnell and the ladies left the V.I.P. section and headed toward the back entrance.

The deejay started spinning the latest hip-hop songs. The bottle ladies returned with the drinks, and King started to drink his Cîroc. After twenty-five minutes of drinking and sidestepping to the music, he realized that Darnell still hadn't returned. Figuring that Darnell was just handling his business for the night, a lady caught his eye. It was Blaze, and she was looking good. Her red hair was in a straight style with razor-sharp bangs, her makeup was flawless, and the see-through sequenced black dress accentuated the curves he didn't know existed. Her red open-toed Manolo Blahniks made her outfit pop. He was in awe of her beauty, then immediately, he became upset. With her was Tee and three guys.

King made a beeline toward the group with fire in his eyes. He saw one of the guys bend down and whisper a few words in Blaze's ear. He made a quick dash and snatched the man by his throat, pushing him back away from Blaze.

"Oh my god, King. What are you doing?" Blaze exclaimed.

"Fuck are you doing? In the club with the next nigga. Is this why you put me out? Huh, so you can be a ho like the rest of your little friends," King bellowed over the music, then glared at Tee with a look that dared her to respond.

"It's not like that. These are Tee's cousins. They are visiting from out of town. Since the four of them were going out, I decided to tag along."

"Tag along? And why the fuck should I care if they are Tee's cousins. They aren't your blood, so you can still wind up fucking these niggas."

"Yo, my man, you are in violation. You need to take it down a notch before we get in your ass."

King punched the dude talking in the mouth, then grabbed Blaze by her arm, dragging her back toward his V.I.P. section.

The group with Tee was too shocked to respond, and Blaze was too embarrassed to care.

The deejay turned the music off, and the lights came on. He announced the management of the club would not tolerate any more fighting. The deejay also warned the next incident would cause the club event to close early.

Before the music came back on, King heard what appeared to be firecracker noises but wasn't sure.

A split second later, one of the women who were with Darnell came running back into the club screaming, *"They are shooting. They are shooting."*

King's heart dropped, but his instincts to survive kicked in. He grabbed Blaze once again by her arm and dragged her toward the nearest exit. As the sounds of the gunshots became closer, he realized there wasn't much time to waste. He picked up Blaze by her hips, placed her over his shoulder, and ran as fast as he could toward Darnell's parked Range Rover.

It was there that his heart stopped. Lying on the car's passenger side was the second woman, Honey, with them earlier and Darnell. Darnell's eyes were staring into space, and there was a gaping hole in the middle of his forehead.

There wasn't any way a person could survive a shot like that. Not wanting to be the next victim, he started to run again with Blaze still on his shoulder. King slowed down his pace when he reached a space that he considered safe. King placed Blaze's feet on the floor, and she grabbed onto him for dear life crying. Never had she been involved in a shoot-out. She was just glad that King was there to help her through the traumatic event.

"Aw damn, they shot my dog," King hollered out, then slid to the floor with his head in the palm of his hands. Tears flowed down his face freely, and Blaze bent down beside him to console him.

"It will be alright, baby," she said softly.

Realizing the gravity of the situation they were still in, he stood up.

"Come on, Blaze. We have to get out of here. No telling if they will start shooting again."

"Wait, what about Tee and them?"

"Man fuck Tee and them niggas. I don't know them. I know and love you.
I'm sure Tee knows enough to run like hell when she hears gunshots. And
if dudes are any type of men, then they know to get her to safety too. Now
let's go," King demanded.

Blaze followed him.

Out of gunfire range, Blaze reached in her Fendi purse for her cell phone.
She had two missed calls from Tee. Relieved, she voice dialed Tee's
number and put the phone on speaker.

"Are you okay, girl?" Tee's voice came blaring through.

"Yes, I just needed to make sure you are safe."

"Yes, I'm safe, girl. Where are you? We'll come back around for you."

"No, need. I'm with her, and I'm taking her home," King interrupted.

"Okay, King. Yawl two get home safely."

Blaze ended the call.

"See what being a follower will get you?" King asked Blaze.

"Please, don't start that shit. Let's just get home where it's safe."

King decided to let the matter drop until they reached home then he would tear into her ass for going out to clubs instead of staying home.

Blaze

Never tell anyone

King and Blaze made it home in no time. Blaze ran into the bathroom to release her bowels. She wasn't only nervous about the shooting but what King was going to say about her being at a club with another man. Tee talked her into going on a date with her cousin. She told Blaze he was a hardworking man who was saving to open his own trucking business.

At first, Blaze was hesitant, but the flashback of seeing King fucking Jazzy on tape ran through her mind numerous times. It was almost giving her PTSD.

Blaze knew she had to get over him. As a result, Blaze figured one date to see if moving on was a possibility wouldn't hurt.

Although King was the only man she slept with, the thought of how fine Tee's cousin was had made her coochie wet. So, tonight she decided to dress as fly as can be. The Blaze was determined to be the best-dressed one in the club.

King's reaction to her attire confirmed her mission was accomplished, but then when the gunshots rang out, all she cared about was here and King making it home safely.

A loud knock on the bathroom door disturbed her thoughts.

"Yo, you good?" King screamed out.

"Yea, just using the bathroom."

King opened the door without further conversation, stared at her on the toilet, and then attacked her verbally.

"You sure were a fucking sight to see tonight. Out here in these streets with niggas you don't know. What type of wife behavior is that?"

"Huh, are you serious, King?"

"What the fuck do you mean asking if I am serious? I say what I mean and ask what the fuck I want to know. Now I want an answer."

"You aren't my father. You can't just say shit and expect that I *have* to answer you. I've been a wife since I met you, but you never appreciated that. All the fucking different bitches, and you get mad about a nigga I didn't even fuck. One I didn't care to fuck. Like I told you earlier, we were just going out to have a bit of fun."

"Fun then fucking afterward."

"Jazzy."

"What? Jazzy what?"

"Nothing, just wanted to remind you about your bitch Jazzy. Now get the fuck out of the bathroom so I can shower."

King didn't listen. Instead, he went to the shower and turned it on. He made sure the water was the temperature she liked, then he stepped back and told her to take her clothes off.

"What? Get out. I can bathe myself."

"I want to see if the coochie's been disturbed."

"Wait? Are you serious right now?"

"Yep, as serious as cancer. Now let's go."

"No, I'm not you or the bitches you be fucking. You know I don't sleep around. I'm faithful, and I always have been."

"Prove it."

"I don't have to prove shit. You should just know it. I mean, when have I ever given you the idea I've been jumping in the sheets with other men," Blaze cried in disbelief.

"You do a lot of talking and no proving. When I say prove it, I mean it. Now take your clothes off before I take them off for you."

"King, you can't be serious right now."

"But I am. Now I want to see your shit so take your fucking clothes off," King bellowed, taking steps towards her.

Blaze jumped off the toilet, turned around, and told him to unzip her dress.

"That's better," King stated as he unzipped the dress.

Blaze stepped out of her shoes then came out of her dress.

"I can't see shit. Take those thongs off."

"Damn, I can't believe this."

"Bitch, are you hiding something?"

"No, but I mean your cousin is lying dead, and you are worrying about if I fucked somebody. I just can't believe this shit right now."

"Don't worry about my cousin right now. You worry about what the fuck I told you to do."

Blaze took her thong off then proceeded to spread her legs. King took his hand and cuffed her pussy. He inserted one finger in then moved it around. He pulled it out when he was satisfied then smelled it.

"Alright, we are good here. Get in the shower."

Blaze, still in disbelief, did as instructed. King left out the bathroom, closing the door. Blaze cried as the hot water hit her face. She couldn't believe how her night had turned out.

After showering Blaze put on her pink cotton bathrobe and joined King in the living room.

She could tell he had been crying. She left the bathroom events behind her and focused on his well-being. After all, his cousin was just viciously murdered.

"Listen," Blaze began.

"No, you listen. No wife of mine is to be seen out in these streets such as you were. You are a beautiful, strong, intelligent woman. Niggas nowadays will only use you up. You deserve the best in life, and I'm the one to give it to you," King said sternly, staring in her dark eyes.

"I just want to be sure you are alright. Your cousin was killed tonight. I shouldn't be your main focus. Have you spoken to his mom?"

"No, I don't know what to say. I'm not even sure the police contacted her yet."

"So why don't we go over there. She shouldn't get this type of news on her own."

"See what I mean, Blaze. You are different. You are selfless. So worried about someone you don't know."

"I'm a person who loves you unconditionally. Therefore, I love those who are connected to you. I just know that you are hurting. So, I know they will be hurting as well."

"I am sorry, baby. You are not only right but exceptional. Put some clothes on. We are going to Aunt Doris's house."

"Okay," Blaze got up and dressed in a pair of light blue jeans with a lavender short sleeve top and purple and white air max on her feet. She was determined to put the night behind her and decided to work things out with King.

But first, they had to be by his aunt Doris's side. Darnell was her only child. Now he was gone. That couldn't be easy to process by herself. No matter how shocked Blaze was, she was determined to be faithful to her husband, but she wouldn't tell anyone what occurred in the bathroom. Not even Tee, her best friend.

King

Recognize a snake when I see one

The night was a mess. Between seeing his wife with another man in the club and seeing his cousin's lifeless body sprawled across the concrete, King was distraught. However, being raised not to show emotions, he faced the task of informing Darnell's mother her son was dead without showing emotions.

Blaze held onto his hand for dear life as they made their way to his black Mercedes. The couple drove the thirty-five minutes in silence.

As King parked the car, a lone tear streamed down King's face. He tried to wipe it off casually, but Blaze noticed.

"It's okay to cry," she began.

"I'm good."

"The problem with black men nowadays is that they don't show emotion. You all carry the world on your shoulders without appreciation and are told it's weak or too feminine when you show vulnerability. Baby, he was your cousin. Your best friend. He was your blood, and it's okay to cry tears over his death. Don't feel insecure or weak to cry," Blaze encouraged.

"I said I am fine. Now just leave it alone. I've bigger fish to fry."

King got out of the car and headed toward his aunt's house without waiting for Blaze. She struggled out of the seat belt then ran to catch up to him.

King stopped outside of his aunt's front door and dropped his head. He took a deep breath then banged on the door. It took about three minutes before he heard the shuffle of his aunt Doris's slippers. She opened the door securing the belt to her green bathrobe.

"Boy, it's you? I was about to take somebody's head off. Do you know what time it is?" Doris asked, bothered.

"Yes, aunt Doris. May we come in?"
Aunt Doris hesitated to stare at King and then Blaze. Her heart sank as she

looked around again, realizing King was the one who went partying with Darnell for his birthday.

"King, where's Darnell?" she asked, knowing something was wrong.

King gently pushed past his aunt. Blaze followed suit.

"Sit down, aunty."

"No, where's Darnell?" she asked firmly.

"Sorry, Aunt Doris, but Darnell won't be showing up. He was shot outside the club."

"Shot, oh my god. I have to get to the hospital. Why didn't the hospital call me? Which one is he in?"

"Aunty, listen to me good. Darnell has been shot. He's gone," King said, then watched in horror and sorrow as his aunt slid to the floor screaming, *"No."*

"I'm sorry," Blaze whispered, going over to assist King with picking up aunt Doris from the floor.

The couple helped aunt Doris to the sofa, where she became hysterical crying. She was beyond distraught.

"Is there anyone you would like me to call aunty?" King asked.

"Yes, call them motherfuckers that killed my baby. This is war," aunt Doris said seriously.

"Now, Ms. Doris, let's let the police handle this. We don't know who shot him anyway," Blaze said, trying to be the voice of reason.

"Man fuck all that," Aunt Doris said. "I believe in an eye for an eye, and those motherfuckers stole my eyesight from me."

"Aunt Doris, let's just worry about making the funeral arrangements and things. I need to do some leg work to find out what happened. He could have just been an innocent bystander," King told a half-lie. He knew in his heart he would get down to the bottom of who shot his family and why. His instincts told him this was more than a lick, and the headshot made things seem personal. He would start by finding the girl who ran into the club screaming when Darnell got shot. "Hey, aunt Doris, when you get Darnell's belongings, I'm going to need his phone."

"For what?" she cried.

"I'm going to need it to start seeing who he had problems with and then take it from there."

As King kept talking to aunt Doris about his plans to find Darnell's killers, there was a loud banging on the door.

It was the police to speak with aunt Doris and make the death notification regarding Darnell.

"Act like we don't know anything, aunt Doris. I don't want to be listed as a witness and questioned. It's important to keep my name out of it so I can do my own investigating."

"I understand, nephew."

After the detectives informed aunt Doris of Darnell's death, she closed the door and turned to King.

"What am I going to do without my baby?" she questioned.

"I know this is hard, but I will be here as much as I can for you, aunty. I promise," King assured her.

The three sat in silence for what seemed like hours. Each had its thoughts. Aunt Doris was thinking of burying her child while King thought of finding and torturing the people responsible for Darnell's death. The headshot made it seem personal to King, and so now it was personal to him. Whoever killed his cousin had better watch their backs. Shit was about to get hectic.

King

Fire in His Eyes

King and Blaze sat with aunt Doris for hours. King kept himself busy by cooking breakfast. He made vegan sausages with hash browns, biscuits, and gravy. Aunt Doris had a juicer so he grabbed a few apples and pears from the fruit basket she kept on the dining room table and made magic happen. After making everyone's plate he called the ladies into the kitchen. They all sat in silence for a few moments. Aunt Doris's eyes were filled to the brim with tears. She kept her head low feeling defeated.

"This looks good baby, " Blaze said breaking the silence.

"Thank you, " King replied. Not ready for making small talk he shoved a sausage in his mouth. He knew Blaze hated when people talked with their mouths full so she would take the hint and quiet down.

"You know what I hate most?" aunt Doris asked.

"What aunt Doris?" King responded.

"The fact I wasn't there to protect him."

"In a situation such as this, there's not much anyone could have done, " King started.

"You know what King? How do you know so much? I mean you show up here and tell me my baby is dead before the police notify me. Now you telling me that there is no way he could have been saved. So my question remains how are you still standing yet Darnell is dead? And on his birthday out of all days? Help me make sense of this all?" she said breaking down in tears.

King reiterated the events of the night to her without leaving any details out while Blaze gently rubbed aunt Doris's back.

"Well, obviously that bitch who ran back in the club had something to do with it. That's the girl I want you to find and torture first!" aunt Doris commanded meaning every word.

"Understood, aunt Doris. Understood, " King confirmed.

Blaze looked on but never said a word. Her eyes were inquisitive but she knew not to say anything doubtful to King at this time. The fire was in his eyes and he didn't care who opposed his upcoming actions. People were going to pay for touching one of his family members.

Blaze

It ain't hard to tell

King and Blaze left aunt Doris's house the next day. She seemed to be in better spirits although this couldn't be easy on her. King thought aunt Doris may have just been putting on a brave face. He and Blaze hoped that she did give him Darnell's cell phone and not try to take matters into her own hands. Aunt Doris was a bold woman not afraid to speak her mind. Neither was she afraid to put action behind her words. They would hate for her to go on a vendetta mission without King to back her but the couple also knew that if decided to there'd be nothing one can do to stop her.

Once at home King decided to step into the shower to cleanse his energy and wash off the sullenness of the previous days' events. He made the water as hot as his skin could stand it then stepped in. Shortly afterward Blaze came in, undressed, and stood behind him wrapping him up in her arms. Her gentle and welcomed embrace caused his tough exterior to melt. The tears began to flow and she held onto King for dear life.

Blaze released King once she heard his breathing become lighter. Grabbing a bar of Black girl magic soap that she ordered from Sugarverse BB she lathered up his washrag and began to wipe him down.

"I got it, " he replied in a low whisper.

"Let me take care of you, " she demanded.

He had to admit it felt good having her attention. Feeling bad for the way he had been treating her lately he obliged her. Blaze finished her task at hand then dropped to her knees taking his full ten-inch package into her mouth. She deep throated his third leg like never done before. When King climaxed she swallowed every last drop. He felt like seizing and his toes curved just a bit. He felt in a better space then he returned the favor. Washing her gently then rinsing her off, he dropped to his knees and cocked her leg up on the shower wall. She placed one hand on his head and the other on the rod to brace herself as King went to town eating her fat pussy and slurping her juices like it was the last supper he'd have on this earth.

The two finished pleasuring each other, dried off, then climbed into their large bed where they lay naked and spent in each other's arms.

King's phone rang at six in the morning. He was still sleeping heavily so she checked the caller I.d.

It said Plush on the screen so she answered it without a greeting wondering why a chick would be calling her husband at that time.

Plush seemed upset as she didn't hesitate to let off a verbal assault.

"King, this is Plush, you better have a good fucking explanation as to why I haven't heard from you in a few days. We were supposed to meet up. Yet you leave me at the hotel lobby looking stupid as I waited for you! How fucking dare you?"

"Now, I don't know who you are but this is King's wife. I can assure you whatever rendezvous the two of you were planning will not be taking place. Not now or ever. So don't ever think of calling this number again."

"Sis, please. Until your *husband* tells me not to call him then your word doesn't mean shit. I'm fucking him not you so get over yourself."

"Fucking?"

"Yes, fucking sis. It ain't hard to tell. You thought he was faithful? Ha! Anyway, I'll be calling back. I'm not going to do the back and forth with a bird, " Plush stated then hung up.

Blaze was stunned. She looked at King who unbeknownst to her heard every word but faked it as if he was asleep. Blaze wanted to knock him upside his head wondering how many other women he was fucking. If he wasn't in such a poor state over the death of Darnell she definitely would have lost her mind and put his ass out buck naked and all. However, wanting to have compassion and make things work with her husband she let him rest. She just didn't know how many more of his indiscretions she could take.

Blaze looked at King once more but this time he acted like he was snoring. She got out the bed and headed to the living room where she cried her eyes out wondering what she did so wrong in her life for her husband not to truly love her. What Blaze didn't realize that it was his insecurities and false knowledge of manhood that made him treat her this way. Blaze was a beautiful soul inside and out but she had to learn that on her own. Nothing King could or couldn't do would help her to that realization and self-love she was so deserving of.

I'm Not Down for the B.S.

King played sleep for as long as his bladder allowed. After the past few days' events, he didn't want to fight with Blaze. Especially about a girl, he was just tricking on. He didn't see a future with Plush.

He didn't understand at times why he was attracted to other women. Blaze was everything he felt a wife should be. Still, he gave in to his desires for other women.

Seeing Blaze at the club with another man the day his cousin died hurt his pride more than it did his heart. Although he didn't have it in him to be the faithful husband she deserves he didn't want to see her move on with someone else who could love her.

King knew it was selfish and insensitive but that was just in his nature. He decided he would make a conscious effort into trying to be a better husband but in the meantime, he didn't want to hear her mouth.

Not being able to hold his urine any longer he climbed out of the bed, dick-swinging, and headed to the bathroom.

"We have to talk, " came the words he dreaded hearing.

"Damn, let a nigga make it to the toilet."

"Okay, as soon as you finish meet me in the living room, " Blaze said and turned to head to the couch.

King used the bathroom, brushed his teeth, and washed his face.

"Might as get this bullshit over with, " he muttered to himself.

By the time he made it to the living room Blaze was sitting on the red recliner still buck-ass naked, her long legs crossed, and a cigarette dangling from her mouth. Her bright face was flushed red and he knew he was in for one hell of an argument.

"When did you start smoking again?" he questioned her.

"Don't ask me no questions until you can be honest and explain to me why would you marry me if you felt I wasn't woman enough for you?"

"Huh?" was all that King could manage to respond. It wasn't that Blaze's question stumped him it's just that he couldn't immediately think of a lie good enough she'd accept as factual.

"Don't *huh* me! If you can *huh* you can hear. Now tell me why I'm not woman enough for you? Why must women call you all weird hours of the night and morning telling me they are fucking you?"

"That's ludicrous. No one can say that dumb shit and if they did then it's all lies to break us up because they want the lifestyle that you live."

"Lifestyle?"

"Yes, lifestyle. The one I bust my ass to provide for you. The one that allows you to eat out dining on filet mignon, lobster, and gourmet French dishes people find hard to pronounce. The lifestyle that allows you, Birkin, Fendi, and Louis bags whenever you feel like going on shopping sprees, and how about that Range Rover you leave parked because according to you it's just too big and powerful for you to handle the roads? I mean you do have it good. Look at how this place is furnished!" King said getting overly excited.

Blaze was on her feet yelling. Her hands were in King's face as spittle flew from her mouth.

"Yeah well, I don't believe you. I think you are fucking these scallywags. The truth of the matter is I would give all of this up. The *lifestyle you provide* to have a faithful marriage with a man who truly loved me."

"Oh so is that why you were at the club with ole boy? Do you know Tee's cousin? I bet your dumb ass would have fucked him had I not snatched you up!" King said trying to change the subject to her instead of focusing on his infidelities. In his heart, he knew that Blaze wasn't capable of running around on him. Yet he would never admit that out loud to her.

"You know that is nowhere near the truth. You are just trying to be hurtful."

"I'm not too sure about all that. I don't know what has happened to you but you have changed Blaze and I don't think that I like it."

"So you are blaming me for you sticking your dick in other women? King, you can't be serious right now."

"Oh but I am. Let me catch you with another dude again and see what happens to the both of you."

"Don't threaten me. Plus I never gave you a reason not to trust me as you have disrespected our marriage. You have shit on my heart and I don't know how much more I can take of your shenanigans."

"You heard me. I'm going back to bed. I have some business to handle later."

"King, don't walk away from this. We have a serious issue I want to address."

"Address it to yourself. I'm going back to sleep."

"King!!!"

"Blaze, I said leave me alone. I'm not down for the b.s., " King said while turning his back to her and going back to the bedroom.

"Just great, " was all King heard from Blaze as she plopped back down on the recliner and started to cry.

"Whew!" King said as he climbed back into the bed and went to sleep. He knew Blaze wouldn't let the issue go but for now, she'd be silent, and he'd get the rest that he needed.

Blaze

Make an Example of Them

Blaze was amazed by King's ability to deflect his flaws and make the trouble in their marriage her fault.

King could make her question if she was coming or going. She promised herself she'd make their relationship work by any means possible but now she was left questioning that decision.

How many indiscretions would she find out about? She was sitting wondering this for a few hours. It didn't make sense to complain to Tee. Tee tried to help her move on from King by taking her out and meeting a decent man but even that got fucked up.

Blaze sat in deep thought until she heard King in the shower. She was tempted to go speak with him but she knew that would start another intense argument.

Blaze lit another cigarette listening inherently to King's actions. By the time he finished showering and dressing in a pair of loose-fitting but not sagging jeans, a white tee, and the latest Jordan's dripping in his jewelry with just a dash of cologne she was hot under the collar.

She couldn't believe he dared to go out despite their verbal altercation earlier. Blaze figured he would want to won't things out.

Her first instinct was to get in his ass demanding to pick up where the earlier argument ended. Then a thought popped into her mind. She wouldn't argue with him but kill him with kindness. She would hope that he wonder why she was being so nice and stick closer to him thinking she was up to something with another man.

"I'm going out."

"To work?"

"No, I left Otha in charge for a few days. I need to make some inquiries about what Darnell was really into and if there is anyone who had it out for him. Something tells me this is personal and not just a lick went wrong."

"Okay baby, be safe, " Blaze responded nonchalantly.

King looked at her awkwardly for a moment. He couldn't put his finger on it but Blaze never let an argument go so easily.

Usually, she screamed and cried until she wore herself out. Maybe she knew how important it was to him to find his cousin's killer so she wasn't trying to cause another useless scene.

Whatever the case may be King was just happy he didn't have to hear her big mouth and think of extraordinary lies to tell trying to make his stories believable.

Before going out the door he turned back to her and gave her a slight kiss on her forehead.

"I love you, Redd, " he said referring to her hair color.

"Hmm, I know you do, " she said lying through her teeth.

She watched as her husband exited through the front door.

Blaze let out a sigh of relief. She grabbed her phone to call Tee who answered on the first ring.

"Blaze are you alright? I haven't heard from you in a few days."

"I'm good girl. The same bullshit different day is all."

"Now what happened, " Tee asked ready to hear the tea.

"Plush happened. She called King at six in the morning. When I answered the phone she said she was fucking him."

"Girl, not Plush? Tall, dark-skin, with a head full of short, soft curls. She dyes it strawberry blonde from time to time."

"Tee, I don't know that chick. This is my first time when speaking to her."

"Oh okay, well if it is the same girl then she's the hairdresser that lives in Arcadia Apartments in South Vistas. She has a reputation for fucking other people's man so I wouldn't be surprised if that's the same girl."

"Damn, and those are the types King likes over me? A faithful, down ass chick."

" Blaze, sometimes a man just don't know if he's coming or going. If he's up or he's down. In other words, they just don't know the good they have at home until it's gone. So what are you going to do now?"

"You said she lives at Arcadia apartments in South Vistas?"

"Yea, why? What you about to do girl?"

I'm about to go beat her ass for all that shit she was popping on *my husband's* phone."

"Normally, I wouldn't condone this over no dude but I never liked that chick. Now I know why. Come pick my ass up and I will show you exactly where she lives, what car she drives, and how the girl looks."

"Bet, give me an hour to get dressed. I'm ready to ride on her ass!"

"Got it. See you then."

Blaze clicked off the phone then raced to the shower to start getting dressed. She was angry, bitter, and had something to prove. She'd start by making an example out of Plush for all the girls who felt they should impede on her marriage!

Blaze

Whoop a Trick

Usually, Blaze was scared to drive the Range Rover but that day she was fearless. She picked up Tee and headed straight to Arcadia Apartments.

Tee had her drive through the parking lot slowly so she could scope out every vehicle in an attempt to locate Plush's car.

As luck would have it Plush was just parking. So Blaze parked close to the exit and jogged with Tee on her heels to catch Plush before she was able to make it to her building.

"Excuse me, Miss," Blaze said drawing the unexpected lady's attention. Blaze had to admit her competition was pretty. She had on a red v-neck top with a pair of cut-off shorts, and Sandles with heels and fluorescent laces that tied up to her knees. Plush's deeply melanated skin was glistening and her face was beaten to the gawds.

The realization of Plush's beauty heightened Blaze's anger even more.

"Yes?" Plush asked.

"Plush, right?"

"Yes," Plush responded surprised that someone was talking to her and asking her name as if she knew them. Plush's aura was kind of stuck up. She knew she was a beauty which caused jealousy amongst her peers and other women. As a result, She kept her distance from people and not too many knew where she lived.

"Please don't be surprised now. I mean you were on my husband's phone talking a lot of shit about how you were fucking him, were you not?" Blaze asked boldly.

Oh shit!" Plush thought to herself. Blaze wasn't an ugly girl. She was beautiful but standing before her in loose-fitting clothes and sneakers on Plush's instincts told her that Blaze was there for a fight.

Not wanting to seem as nervous as she felt, Plush decided to talk hella shit.

"Don't come here with that ghetto shit trying to check me. It's your husband you need to check."

" Don't worry. He's been checked now it's your turn. See everyone in the world knows he has a wife. Yet your ass decided to disrespect me and my marriage."

"No, your husband did that. Now, I don't have the time for this drama. I'm going to my house and I suggest you go home and fuck your husband as well as I do. Maybe if you did he wouldn't find time to roam the streets looking for bad bitches like me to fuck."

"He fucks you because you're easy but today all that stops."

"Well tell your husband that because he called me earlier saying he wanted to meet up again and you two were separated. See you may be pretty but your pussy is trash. Bye!" Plush said trying to end the conversation. She proceeded to walk past Blaze and continue to her apartment.

Blaze was furious.

"Don't walk away from me!"

"Or what?" was the last thing Plush was able to say before Blaze began to beat the brakes off of her.

Blaze somehow managed to get Plush on the ground and nearly under the car's front hood.

Not being able to stop herself when she saw a bottle on the ground, sitting on top of Plush with one hand wrapped tightly around her neck, Blaze reached for the bottle with her free hand, broke it, and slashed Plush's pretty face.

Plush let out the squeal of horror. Even Tee was taken aback yet too afraid to move. She had seen Blaze fight before but never like this.

"Now see if anyone's husband would want to fuck you after this!" Blaze hollered.

Having seen enough a bystander came and grabbed Blaze off Plush.

Blaze and Tee raced back to the Ranger. Blaze was visibly shaking so Tee thought it was in their best interest for her to drive.

The two rode back in silence until Tee finally said, "Damn, that's how you whoop a trick!"

The pair laughed but unbeknownst to them this wouldn't be the last they would see of Plush, not in the least.

King

Stick Beside Her

King ran a few errands trying to hear what the streets were saying in regards to Darnell being killed.

They were giving a little buzz about a man named Rolando being involved but nothing was concrete.

Since King had been out of the drug and stick up game for a while and was now a successful business owner the name Rolando didn't ring a bell.

He got wind that the lady who survived the shoot-out that night was laying low. Her name was Hennessy. She didn't want to be a witness not did she want to feel the wrath from Rolando or Darnell's people.

Although this may have been the case he was able to track her down at a cousin's house and decided to watch the comings and goings before discussing with her. For some reason, his spidey senses were tingling and he knew he had to be discreet about things. He couldn't have word getting back to Darnell's potential killer or killers that someone was on to him.

It seemed Hennessy was hiding in a trap house. This made his job a bit harder. There wasn't any telling who else might be linked to the murder and who may not.

He watched the comings and goings of the spot for a few hours until he spotted Hennessy with one of Darnell's children's mothers. This became much more intricate than he originally thought.

Could Kandy have had a hand in setting up Darnell? He had to find out and instead of approaching the pair, he followed them.

The duo didn't go anywhere special, just to grab a bite to eat then a beauty salon. King waited patiently when a black Mercedes-Benz pulled up. For some reason, the car seemed familiar.

Kandy walked around to the driver's side and the tinted window rolled down.

"Oh shit, " King whispered. Behind the steering wheel were Cane, Darnell, and his cousin.

King watched intensively as Kandy bent down to kiss Cane on the lips. It was passionate in nature and not just a peck on the cheek.

King continued watching as Cane's dark chocolate hand reached to touch the cleavage revealed through Kandy's V-neck tank top. Her light brown face became flushed and she smiled from ear to ear.

King couldn't help but wonder how long the two have been intimate. King became upset thinking about the way Cane and Kandy was disrespectful to Darnell and his memory.

He wanted to confront them but was glad he waited when he saw a vanilla envelope exchanged. He could bet his life savings that money was involved and it probably had something to do with Darnell's death.

"God, don't tell me Cane and Kandy set my cousin up. I swear I may be retired from the street life but I will damn sure come out of retirement to put these two in an early grave, " King said to himself.

King watched as the two conversed. Hennessy came joined them in their discussion. Kandy giggled at Cane's every word and Hennessy listened intently. It was twenty minutes later when Kandy and Hennessy went back into the beauty salon.

King sat in disbelief, and confusion for a few minutes then drove off to check in on his barbershop figuring he would get a lineup while there.

"Hey bossman, " Rollo said to him as he entered the front door. "We were just speaking on you and wondering if things were okay because we saw Blaze and Plush on the news."

"Huh, Blaze and Plush on the news?"

"Yea, you ain't know?"

"Know what?" King asked confused. At the same time, a news reporter flashed on the 50" inch flat-screen that hung on the wall above the smokey gray-colored wall that the barbers stations were.

"In other news cops have put out an arrest warrant for Blaze Blount, who was caught on tape viciously attacking Claire Plush Battiste of Arcadia Apartments. Another lady was with Blount and she is wanted for questioning as well."

"What the fuck?" King said in disbelief. How did Blaze find Plush to attack her in the first place? Now not only did King have to worry about piecing together his cousin's murder he had to worry about the case Blaze was about to fight in court. Although he was upset Blaze was his wife and he was going to stick beside her during this mess.

King

Stick Beside Her

King ran a few errands trying to hear what the streets were saying in regards to Darnell being killed.

They were giving a little buzz about a man named Rolando being involved but nothing was concrete.

Since King had been out of the drug and stick up game for a while and was now a successful business owner the name Rolando didn't ring a bell.

He got wind that the lady who survived the shoot-out that night was laying low. Her name was Hennessy. She didn't want to be a witness not did she want to feel the wrath from Rolando or Darnell's people.

Although this may have been the case he was able to track her down at a cousin's house and decided to watch the comings and goings before discussing with her. For some reason, his spidey senses were tingling and he knew he had to be discreet about things. He couldn't have word getting back to Darnell's potential killer or killers that someone was on to him.

It seemed Hennessy was hiding in a trap house. This made his job a bit harder. There wasn't any telling who else might be linked to the murder and who may not.

He watched the comings and goings of the spot for a few hours until he spotted Hennessy with one of Darnell's children's mothers. This became much more intricate than he originally thought.

Could Kandy have had a hand in setting up Darnell? He had to find out and instead of approaching the pair, he followed them.

The duo didn't go anywhere special, just to grab a bite to eat then a beauty salon. King waited patiently when a black Mercedes-Benz pulled up. For some reason, the car seemed familiar.

Kandy walked around to the driver's side and the tinted window rolled down.

"Oh shit, " King whispered. Behind the steering wheel were Cane, Darnell, and his cousin.

King watched intensively as Kandy bent down to kiss Cane on the lips. It was passionate in nature and not just a peck on the cheek.

King continued watching as Cane's dark chocolate hand reached to touch the cleavage revealed through Kandy's V-neck tank top. Her light brown face became flushed and she smiled from ear to ear.

King couldn't help but wonder how long the two have been intimate. King became upset thinking about the way Cane and Kandy was disrespectful to Darnell and his memory.

He wanted to confront them but was glad he waited when he saw a vanilla envelope exchanged. He could bet his life savings that money was involved and it probably had something to do with Darnell's death.

"God, don't tell me Cane and Kandy set my cousin up. I swear I may be retired from the street life but I will damn sure come out of retirement to put these two in an early grave, " King said to himself.

King watched as the two conversed. Hennessy came joined them in their discussion. Kandy giggled at Cane's every word and Hennessy listened intently. It was twenty minutes later when Kandy and Hennessy went back into the beauty salon.

King sat in disbelief, and confusion for a few minutes then drove off to check in on his barbershop figuring he would get a lineup while there.

"Hey bossman, " Rollo said to him as he entered the front door. "We were just speaking on you and wondering if things were okay because we saw Blaze and Plush on the news."

"Huh, Blaze and Plush on the news?"

"Yea, you ain't know?"

"Know what?" King asked confused. At the same time, a news reporter flashed on the 50" inch flat-screen that hung on the wall above the smokey gray-colored wall that the barbers stations were.

"In other news cops have put out an arrest warrant for Blaze Blount, who was caught on tape viciously attacking Claire Plush Battiste of Arcadia Apartments. Another lady was with Blount and she is wanted for questioning as well."

"What the fuck?" King said in disbelief. How did Blaze find Plush to attack her in the first place? Now not only did King have to worry about piecing together his cousin's murder he had to worry about the case Blaze was about to fight in court. Although he was upset Blaze was his wife and he was going to stick beside her during this mess.

She was my best friend

Blaze

Blaze was antsy, to say the least. What had seemed to be a good idea went left quickly. However, once she started pummeling Plush with blows she couldn't contain the anger she felt. Next thing she knew she cut Plush with a bottle and was hiding out from not only the law but her husband King.

King showing up to Aunt Doris' house to go with her to the precinct gave her the strength and courage needed to face the judge.

It was a bit of a wait but once she got in front of the judge she was in for the shock of her life.

Tee was already inside and gave a statement against Blaze. Tee told everything about how Blaze planned on fighting Plush.

Tee even added in a few extra details that were all lies. Tee stated that it was Blaze who knew where Plush lived and gave her the belief that she planned to assault Plush for months.

Blaze knew it wasn't looking good on her part and her attorney even had a concerned look on his face.

"Why did she lie like that," Blaze screamed at Mr. Martin hysterically.

"Calm down. We still have a chance at this. I just need to find the holes in her statement," he assured Blaze.

Blaze was shaking visibly. She wasn't punk but she didn't want to be anyone's bitch in jail. Blaze heard the horror stories and she didn't want to encounter any of it.

After further discussion between the prosecutor Mrs. Mitchell and Mr. Martin, and Blaze, Judge Valentine ordered Blaze's bail to be set at seventy-five thousand and for Blaze's passport to be turned in so she didn't pose as a flight risk.

"Although you may not have meant to commit an aggravated assault, you can still be charged with this felony offense. To hear your side of events you admit to committing a misdemeanor assault offense and caused serious injury using a weapon. There may be a variety of other aggravating factors which are yet to be determined.

As a result, a person may be charged with aggravated assault under A.R.S. § 13-1204 (A) if the person knowingly, recklessly, or intentionally provoke, injure, insult, cause physical injury or harm to another person.

Since you have caused serious physical injury to another; and used a dangerous object to use as a weapon this is the court's recourse of action.

You are hereby reprimanded until your bond has been posted.

Good day," Judge Valentine said before giving a court date for three months.

"What does this mean? Tee was lying on me. She gave me Plush's address and drove me there. This isn't fair."

"I know but nothing in life is fair. One must fight for fair treatment but Blaze please don't fret. I'm sure King will have you out in no time."

"I know he will. I honestly don't have any doubts about that but that bitch Tee snaked me. With the video plus Plush and her testimony, I may be sentenced to football numbers. She was my best friend. How could she do me like that?"

"This may be easier said than done but please don't worry yourself. Let King bail you out and we will all meet at my office in a few days. I have a few tricks up my sleeve to fight this case. Now, do you understand me?"

"Yes," Blaze whispered to Mr. Martin as court officials came to assist her back to the holding cell.

Tears flowed down her face as King watched the court's monitor in a hot rage.

It would be a few hours before he could get the money to bail Blaze out. Thoughts of murdering Tee entered his mind. As good of a friend as Blaze was to Tee he couldn't for the life of him figure out why she took the lying route instead of having Blaze's back.

However, he knew that Tee was the least of his worries first thing first was getting his wife home.

Blaze

No Place Like Home

Once Blaze was released King sped to the nearest McDonald's. Usually, the pair ate healthy meals but today wasn't one of those days.

The couple ordered pancakes and eggs without the sausage and orange juice to wash it down.

They are in the parking lot while Blaze gorged her food as if it was her first meal in months.

"Whoa, slow down killer. We have food at the house if you are still hungry after this, " King half-joked.

"I feel as if I haven't eaten in months, " Blaze admitted. "They only had dry-ass bologna sandwiches with a thick-ass slice of cheese and half-rotten white milk."

"All the taxes we pay and that's what inmates get to eat?" King asked.

"Yea well not all inmates are innocent as they proclaim. So, I understand why even if I don't agree with it."

"Hmm, you finished eating. I'm ready to get you home so you can take those clothes off and burn them."

"Burn them?" Blaze asked a bit stumped.

"Yes, burn them. It's an old superstition. If you burn the clothes you were arrested in you won't return to jail."

"Burn them it is!" Blaze giggled. King's heart was overjoyed that during this time he could make her happy.

Then the inevitable came up.

"Can you believe that bitch Tee? I can't wrap my mind around how she could make a statement against me."

"Now you see why I always had a shaky feeling about her?"

"Yes, I could. I just never thought she would do this to me."

"Remember this Blaze...betrayal usually comes from those we love. That's why it hurts most. But I don't want you to get stuck in victimization mode. When she comes crawling back, because that's what snakes and rats do, don't ever forget how she made you feel. Don't forget this feeling. Just know she did that shit and she meant it. If you are ever her friend again then what she does next is on you, not her. Do you understand me?"

"Yes, but I just want to kick her ass one good time."

"Your best revenge is walking away and stacking your paper. Please know she did this pit of jealousy and fear. She is not the friend you thought she was. Plus kicking her ass will land you back in jail. Just move on. That will cit bee most."

"I understand baby and I will try my best."

"Don't try...do!"

"I will."

"Good, now let's get home and get you out of those clothes. You are stinking up my vehicle smelling like lock-up, " King joked.

The two had a good laugh pulling into traffic. Once home Blaze raced for the bathroom, stripped, and jumped in the shower.

King grabbed her clothes and burned them in the backyard while making sure there weren't any neighbors around.

When he returned inside Blaze was in the bed buck naked waiting on him.

King devoured her body. Starting with eating her push first then entering her slowly. The pair made love for hours, cumming over and over again until they lay spent in each other's arms.

"There's no place like home in your arms, "Blaze whispered softly. Then she fell into a deep, restful sleep while king held onto her tightly never wanting her to leave his side again.

After laying with her in his arms for hours, King got up, put on a pair of silk pajamas, and headed for the kitchen.

There he prepared a Caesar salad topped with fruit and garlic knots. He made some homemade sorrel. Then set the table with one white candle placed in the middle.

King went back into the bedroom.

"Rise and shine sleepyhead, " he said shaking her gently.

Blaze woke.

"What happened baby?"

"Nothing, I just don't want you to sleep all day. Wash the crust out your eye and meet me in the kitchen."

"Okay baby. Whatever you say."

Blaze stayed naked. She had no problem letting her bare ass hanging out in front of the man she loved.

She came to life as she smelled her favorite garlic knots. When she entered the kitchen the one white candle and dim lights enhanced the atmosphere.

King was so thoughtful and attentive during her time of trouble. She ran over to him and kissed him feverishly.

"Sit and eat. We will have days to make love interrupted. I am taking time off indefinitely."

"Can we afford that, " Blaze asked genuinely concerned. King handled all the finances so at times she didn't know what was going on with their finances."

"Let me worry about that. Just know I'm not fiscally irresponsible. If I say I'm taking time off then yes we can afford it. Besides helping you out of this jam, I still have to make time to fulfill my promise to aunt Doris. Got me?"

"Yes, I do and I am so very glad you are a man of your word. That's why you are the King."

"You better know it."

The two are making small talk in between bites. When they finished their food they sat in the living room watching television until the need to make love hit them once more.

King chased Blaze into the bedroom with her giggling all the way.

Blaze was happy to be home and more than happy to be married to King. She wanted nothing to ruin this moment and by the grace of God, it wouldn't.

You already knew that!

King and Blaze, were bored and tired of staying in the house. Despite the pandemic there were a few places they could wine and dine at. The couple decided to go to a quaint Asian place. The atmosphere was euphoric and Blaze felt like a queen as the table chef prepared their order in front of them.

Blaze giggled thinking of the 'Infamous Salt Bae.'

"What's tickling you?" King inquired.

"Oh, nothing, " Blaze responded giggling.

"If you say so, " he said not wanting to press the issue. The mood was light and he didn't want to ruin it with foolishness and his insecurities.

The couple made small talk until the food was served. They dug into their cuisine when hearing a familiar voice.

"Tee-Tee!" they said in unison. Blaze's face turned a beet red as she spotted Tee-Tee with a caramel complexioned chick she'd never seen before.

"Just keep calm and ignore her."

"How can I? She betrayed me."

" That's partly true but let this be a lesson always do your dirt by yourself."

"You're right. It's just sad that it may cost me my freedom."

"Yea, well you got this. The lawyer is a bulldog in court and if he can't get you off I know someone who can beat the charges in appeal. Don't you worry, understand me?"

"Yea but..."

Boom.. "Oh excuse me," Tee Tee said purposely bumping into King and Blaze's table.

"Ain't no excuse me bitch. You saw us sitting here, " Blaze hissed turning beet-red while King steadied himself to grab Blaze in case she jumped up from the chair ready to whoop Tee-Tee's ass.

"Did you call me a bitch? Are you sure that's how you want to come at me?"

"Why wouldn't I? You think I'm scared of you? You see a sista got hands."

"And weapons. You ain't nothing but a punk and I almost caught charges because of you. Of course, I was going to save my own ass. Fuck you ever do for me to owe you such loyalty?"

"It's called friendship bitch, " Blaze hollered losing her composure.

King tried to intercede because things were become g two heated between the former best friends.

"That's enough Blaze. We know you aren't a punk and will beat the brakes off her BUT you have an open case. Right now deal with that and all else can come later."

Blaze was seething. All she saw was red. There was an undeniable fire in her eyes. She was ready to attack Tee-Tee and King knew it.

"Tee-Tee, you've said and done enough. Why don't you and your friend keep it moving."

"Yea you would take her side."

"What do you mean by that? Blaze is my wife. Her side will always be my priority."

"Yea, well it wasn't a priority when you were digging Plush and my back out a few weeks ago."

"What? What did you just say?" Blaze asked confused.

Blaze knew what she heard come from Tee-Tee's mouth but it didn't make sense.

If Tee-Tee was correct then King wasn't only a serial cheater but a dirty dog that fucked who she thought was her ride -or-die best friend.

"You heard me."

"No, repeat that."

"Blaze, she's lying. I swear I ain't touch her. Not in that way."

"Oh, not in that way King? What the fuck does that mean? How did you fucking touch her?" Blaze yelled as on-lookers intently stared at the quartet and the trouble that brewed.

"Yo, mane quit while you're ahead, " one bald, dark-skinned man with a long beard said knowing King was about to talk his way into a divorce.

King ignored him and reached for Blaze's hand. She pulled away from him then hauled off and smacked the shit out of him.

King saw stars and orbs. Had it been anyone else, no matter if they were male or female, he would have laid hands on them.

"Happy now?" King asked Tee-Tee as Blaze rushed to the nearest exit.

Tee-Tee and her unknown friend watched as Blaze exited the restaurant in a mad dash.

Tee-Tee turned her attention back to King and said, "Now I'm happy!" And her and her tag-a-long let out a wicked laugh.

"Blaze is right...you are a bitch, " King started.

"But you already knew that!" Tee-Tee said then walked away leaving King standing there with tears forming in his eyes